My Fairytale Time

Goldilocks and the Three Bears

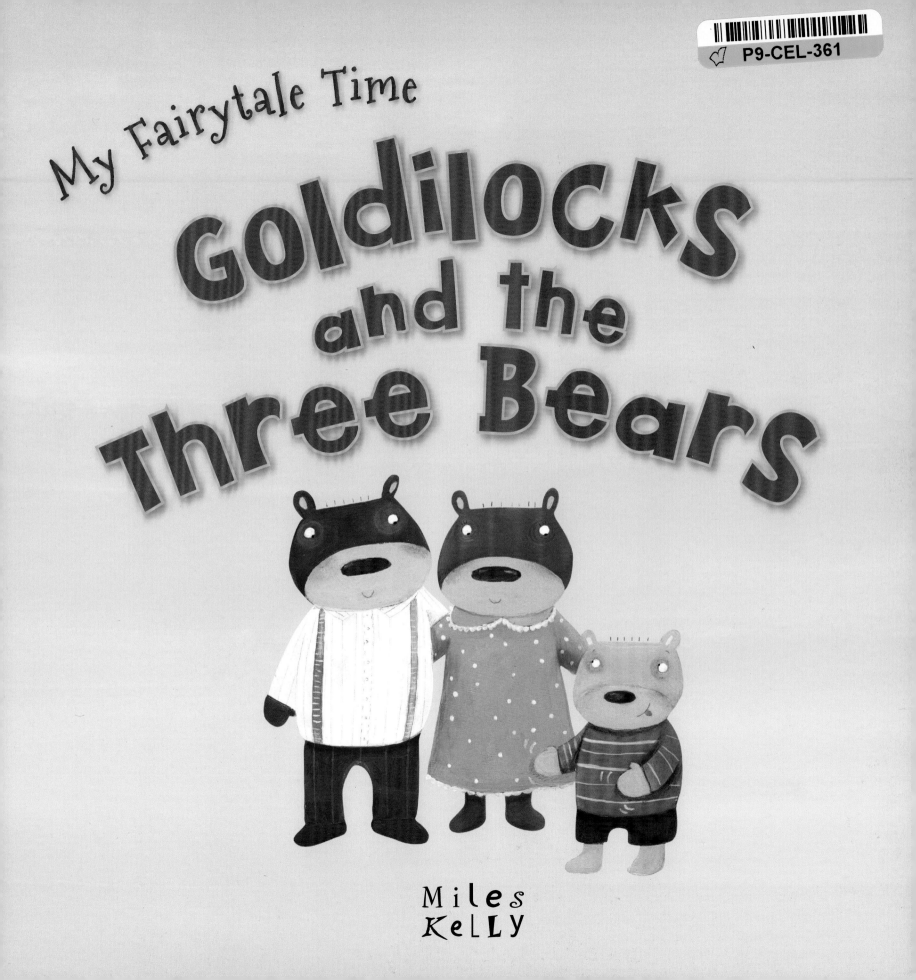

Miles Kelly

Once upon a time, there were **three bears** who lived in a house on the edge of a wood.

There was Father Bear,
Mother Bear and
little Baby Bear.

Every day, the bears had porridge for breakfast. But one morning they found it was far too hot to eat.

"Let's go for a walk in the wood while the porridge cools down," said Father Bear.

A little girl called Goldilocks was also walking in the wood that day. She had wandered too far from home while playing.

At last Goldilocks came across the bears' house. The door was open, so she went in to have a look around.

Goldilocks saw the three bowls. She tried porridge in the biggest bowl, but it was too lumpy. The medium-sized bowl was too sweet. But the porridge in the smallest bowl was just right.

Too lumpy!

Too sweet!

Just right!

So she ate it
ALL up.

Too hard!

After eating the porridge, Goldilocks decided to explore. She went into the living room, where she saw three chairs.

She sat in the **biggest** chair, but it was too hard. The **medium-sized** chair was too soft. So Goldilocks tried the **smallest** chair.

Too soft!

Whoops!

The smallest chair was just right. But all of a sudden... CRASH! it broke into pieces.

All of a sudden Goldilocks felt **very tired.** She went upstairs to find somewhere to sleep.

There were three beds in a big bedroom. Goldilocks tried each of them, and found that the smallest bed was just right.

She fell
fast asleep.

"I'm starving!"

When the three bears arrived home they were very hungry. But something wasn't right. "Someone's been eating my porridge," growled Father Bear.

"Someone's been eating my porridge," said Mother Bear. "Someone's been eating MY porridge," cried Baby Bear.

"And they've eaten it all up!"

The bears went into the living room. "Someone's been sitting in my chair," growled Father Bear. "Someone's been sitting in my chair," said Mother Bear.

"Someone's been sitting in MY chair," wailed Baby Bear.

"And they've broken it!"

Stomp stomp stomp!

Together, the three bears marched upstairs to investigate.

"Someone's been sleeping in my bed!" roared Father Bear.
"And in my bed, too!" cried Mother Bear.

"Someone's been sleeping in my bed," squealed Baby Bear. "And she's still there!" Goldilocks awoke to see the three bears.

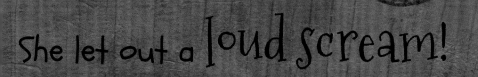

She let out a loud scream!

AAARGH!

Goldilocks leapt out of bed and ran down the stairs. She ran all the way home. And what did the bears do? They made some **more porridge!**